MURDER
ON
MARS

First published in 2000 by Franklin Watts
A division of the Watts Publishing Group Limited
96 Leonard Street, London EC2A 4XD

Copyright © Franklin Watts 2000

Editor in Chief: John C. Miles
Designer: Jason Anscomb
Consultant: Robin Kerrod

A CIP catalogue record for this book
is available from the British Library.

ISBN   0 7496 3470 7 (hbk)
       0 7496 3474 X (pbk)

Printed in Great Britain

2

MURDER ON MARS

BY
MICHAEL
JOHNSTONE

ILLUSTRATIONS
BY ANDY DIXON

W
FRANKLIN WATTS
NEW YORK • LONDON • SYDNEY

Let's think for a moment about your great-grandfather. He was probably born in the 1880s or 1890s. It is quite likely he worked in a factory or, if he was lucky, in an office where he would spend his days hand-copying columns of figures into a big book. Occasionally he may have been caught daydreaming about being rich enough to own a new-fangled motorcar. A few years later, he might have talked excitedly to his friends about two American brothers who had actually flown in the first manned, powered aeroplane.

You were more than likely born in the 1980s or 1990s. You are probably driven to school each day. You almost certainly have a calculator that can do complicated sums in a fraction of a second. Your computer can give you access to millions of facts and, at the press of a button, let you send a message around the world.

If he could see what the world was like now, your great-grandfather would scratch his head in wonder. And so would you if, Rip-Van-Winkle-like, you went to sleep today and woke up in a hundred years.

What will the world be like then?

Given how much things have changed in the last century, it's almost impossible to answer that question.

Almost. But not quite.

For scientists all over the world are designing next-generation technology that will make Moon travel as everyday as a flight to New York is today. Technology that will make it possible to travel to Mars and to live and work there too.

So step into the future with us. Enjoy a murder mystery set on Mars at the end of the twenty-first century and then, once it's solved, learn a little about the technology of tomorrow's world.

MURDER ON MARS

I was in my office when the call came through.

'Yes!' I snapped into my voice mike, my eyes fixed firmly on my computer screen.

'Miss Stravinsky?' I didn't recognize the voice.

'Not really,' I said. 'He was a lousy composer!'

'Sorry?'

'Forget it!' I sighed. 'Just a joke. This is Stravinsky. Who am I talking to?'

'Jack Nairn Security!' The words were rushed.

'And what can I do for you, Mr Security?'

'It's Nairn. Jack Nairn. From Security.'

Hello! Anyone on this planet ever strung the words 'of', 'sense' and 'humour' together and come up with a useful phrase?

'Sorry, Mr Nairn. What can I do for you?'

'Could you come to Commander Kun's office?' He sounded brisk and efficient. 'He needs to talk to you right away.'

My right hand clicked on the mouse and moved it around, highlighting the back-up fuel system of the nuclear-powered rocket engine outlined on my screen. Voice- and touch-activated screens were all very well, but for real intricate work there is nothing to beat a good old-fashioned mouse. It gives you more control. At least that's what I thought; and having become the Interplanetary Energy Agency's youngest ever Director of Rocketry and Rocket Research, I couldn't be that far wrong.

My dad had been using a voice-reactive computer when he had been monitoring nuclear power generation on the experiment he had been working on that day almost a year ago. If he had been using a mouse some people think he'd still be alive.

'What does he want to talk to me about?'

'I'm afraid he doesn't tell me things like that,' Jack Nairn sighed.

'Couldn't he use the video link?' I asked, shading the exhaust nozzle blue.

'You're not the only one I've been instructed to call to his office.'

'There are conference facilities on the link.' I moved the cursor up, clicked the mouse and watched lines of figures unroll down the left side of the screen.

'Miss Stravinsky.' If my uncooperative attitude was getting to Jack Nairn, it wasn't obvious from his pleasant, friendly voice. 'Please make your way to Commander Kun's office right away.' And with a soft click, my earphones went dead.

I sighed as I saved what was on screen. That done, I switched off my headset, pulled it over my hair and dangled it over the ever-present bottle of mineral water by the left side of my keyboard. Pushing my too-thick fringe to one side, I left my laboratory and headed for Kun's office. As I went I told myself to make an appointment to have my hair cut asap.

I liked Kun. He'd been at the final vetting session of my selection process when he had impressed me with the cool, precise way he'd asked his questions.

No wasted words.

He had come straight to the point. 'Have the circumstances of your father's death influenced the way you approach your work, Miss Stravinsky?'

'Yes, sir.' I'd held his steely gaze quite steadily. 'It has taught me you can never be too careful when dealing with nuclear reaction. If a man as experienced as my father can make such a simple, fatal mistake, then no one can be too careful.'

'Good!'

And that had been that.

The next time we'd met had been at the

reception held in my honour shortly after I had taken up my appointment a few weeks later.

'Welcome to Mars, Miss Stravinsky,' he had said. 'I'm looking forward to working with you.'

I was about to say I was looking forward to being part of the team, when Lars Aschengreen tapped him on the shoulder and drew him into a conversation from which I was excluded. I stood there like a lemon until Kun stopped the tall, blond Dane in mid-sentence. 'Have you met Ms Stravinsky yet, Lars?'

'Ah. So you are she.' Aschengreen ran his pale blue eyes over me and said, 'You look more like your mother than your father.'

'She has her father's brains,' Kun smiled at me.

'Indeed.' Aschengreen nodded curtly. 'Excuse me. There is someone over there I must talk to,' he said, turning on his heels.

'Is he always so rude?' I tried to laugh.

'You should see him when he's trying,' Kun raised an eyebrow. 'He doesn't so much rub people up the wrong way as kick 'em there. He's got more enemies here than the last man-eating tiger had in India.'

'Didn't the last man-eating tiger in India end up strung up between two trees?' I frowned. 'That's hardly likely to happen to the Agency's Director and Chief Executive of Martian Operations.'

'True!' Kun had laughed. 'But only because there are no trees on Mars.'

No sooner had I swiped my smart card through the entry system than the door slid open and I stepped into Jiri Kun's outer office.

'Miss Stravinsky,' said the dark-haired young man sitting with his back to a bank of screens. 'Please go straight through.'

'Thanks,' I said and made my way across the room towards the door he was pointing at.

When I was about half a metre away, it opened automatically. 'Sorry I took so long,' I said, acknowledging the nods that greeted me. 'But at least I'm not last,' I waved at the empty chair between Jiri Kun and Lydia Kyasht, Head of Resource Management, as I took my seat.

All the other heads of department were there.

'Director Aschengreen will not be joining us,' Charles Lisner, the good-looking Australian in charge of engineering operations said softly,

'Oh, of course.' I gently snapped a finger against my thumb and looked round the table. 'He's on the Deimos project, isn't he? Good! That should make this a more pleasant meeting.'

The silence that followed my remark was so

intense that when I swallowed I half expected to hear an echo. Everyone cast their eyes downwards, avoiding making eye contact with me.

'There has been an accident,' Jiri Kun cut through the quiet. 'Mr Aschengreen is dead.'

'Dead!' I slumped back in my chair. 'What . . . I . . . When . . .' I managed to gasp before my mouth dried up and I reached for the tumbler of water in front of me. 'What sort of accident?' I croaked.

'The shuttle he and the others were in exploded shortly after take-off from *Olympus Mons*,' said Lilo Gruber, the ultra-efficient German in charge of transport. 'Everyone aboard was killed.' She could have been asking the time for all the emotion there was in her voice.

'When did this happen?' I leaned forward, put my elbows on the table and clasped my hands together. 'I mean, how long into the flight were they?'

'Take-off plus forty,' said Matz Borlin, my great buddy among the other heads of department. Matz, a great blond Viking of a man, was the only Norwegian I had ever met who had anything approaching a sense of humour. But this was no time for laughter: his voice was sombre.

'What happened?' I asked. 'I mean what caused their shuttle to blow up?' I looked at Lilo. 'All spacecraft are serviced once a month and checked before each mission, aren't they?'

'And again when they get back,' she said.

'Then how could it have exploded?' I furrowed my brow, as if I was asking myself the question and trying to come up with the answer, like my grandad used to do when he couldn't find his glasses.

'That's what we want you to find out.' Kun nodded in my direction. 'The most likely explanation is a malfunction in one of the rockets. And as Director of Rocketry – '

He let the rest of his sentence hang in the air.

'Of course,' I said. 'I'll make arrangements to travel to the site of the accident right away.'

'Wouldn't it be a more efficient use of your time to have the wreckage brought to you here?' Lilo Gruber peered at me over the top of her half-moon glasses.

'It will be much faster if I go there rather than wait here,' I said quickly. 'And if I can fly over the wreckage and see how it's dispersed, I should be able to get a pretty good initial idea of what may have gone wrong.'

'How?' Lilo asked.

'Well,' I said, trying to keep an edge from my voice, 'if it was a malfunction in the immediate-post-ignition system I would expect fragments to be scattered in a more circular pattern than if it was a failure in the post-launch secondary booster rockets.'

'Less costly staff could easily take aerial

photographs of the site.' You'd have thought Lilo paid the wages bill out of her own pocket.

I sighed and let my chin rest on my hands, looked round the table and said, 'In cases like this, the human eye is more efficient than the camera. Especially an experienced human eye like mine.

'Also,' I went on before anyone could interrupt, 'I don't want anyone touching the wreckage before I do. They may accidentally destroy vital clues.'

'Very well,' said Kun, who, I remembered, had automatically assumed control now that Aschengreen was dead. 'Make arrangements to travel to the accident site as quickly as possible.'

'Thank you,' I smiled. 'I'll make the preliminary survey on my own.'

'I'd like you to take an assistant with you.'

'I'd rather go on my own.'

'I insist!'

I shrugged my shoulders. 'In that case I'll take John Meehan my Number Two along.'

'No!' Kun said the word sharply. 'I'd like you to take Jack Nairn.'

Jack Nairn? I'm about to set out on what could be one of the most vital missions in my life and he wants me to take a secretary along?

A saying of my dad's came to mind.

'No way, José!'

'So how do you like being on Mars, Nairn?' I asked as we made our way to the *Pathfinder* Hangar a short ride from Headquarters.

'I like it very much, Miss Stravinsky.'

'If we have to work together, you can drop the Miss,' I said.

'Just Stravinsky?'

'I do have a first name, it's – '

'Dianne-Doris,' Nairn interrupted. 'Commander Kun told me.'

'He should also have told you that the last person to call me that ended up with a very sore mouth,' I snarled. 'It's DeeDee! Got that? DeeDee.'

'Right, DeeDee.' Nairn turned and smiled at me. A tiny gold filling in one of his front teeth was the only flaw in a set that could have starred in a toothpaste ad. 'And I'm Jack. Short for –'

'Jacobite!' I said. 'Commander Kun told me.'

'One of the last people to call me that ended up with a black eye.' He grinned. 'And I ended up with this,' he went on, pointing at the filling.

'Must have been quite a scrap!'

'It was.' That grin again. 'I broke his jaw as well.'

Funny, I'd fought tooth and nail not to have Jack Nairn tag along with me on the mission, and even before we'd set off I was starting to like him.

My big mistake had been to try to argue that I didn't need a junior secretary with me.

Even before the word 'secretary' was out of my mouth, Kun had cut me short and told me that Jack Nairn was no ordinary secretary. He was a High Flier.

And when he'd told me that, I knew I might as well try to land an ice cube on the Sun as try to stop Nairn accompanying me.

High Fliers are the cream of university graduates in their year. And when I say cream I mean C-R-E-A-M. The Agency bends over backwards to recruit these young men and women who could walk into any job they chose at the flick of a finger.

Once recruited they spend time working in various divisions of the Agency to acquire an all-round picture of its operations. Then they are given a job in their own specialist fields.

'You know how much importance the Agency puts on High-Flier training,' Kun had said.

'You should,' Lilo Gruber had cut in. 'You were a High Flier yourself.'

'Why wasn't I told about him?' I snapped.

'Don't you ever read your e-c file?' One day I'm going to do serious damage to Lilo Gruber. 'His appointment was confirmed in electronic communication 787/7, dated – '

'All right! All right! All right.' I know when I'm

beaten. 'I'll take him along.'

And as I said, there I was a few hours later starting to like Jack Nairn.

Liking him was one thing. Wanting him peering over my shoulder and asking all sorts of questions was another thing altogether. I wanted to get this investigation over as quickly as possible and then get back to the new nozzle design I was working on.

'What did you major in?' I asked him as our transporter approached the air lock at the mouth of the glass-lined tunnel that led to *Pathfinder*. I was making conversation, for I already knew the answer: the first thing I'd done when I had got back to my office after that meeting with Kun was to catch up on e-c 787/7.

Was Jack Nairn intelligent?

Had the blue whale been hunted to extinction eighty years ago?

He had more letters after his name than there were in the alphabet.

'Nuclear Ergo-Aeronautical Techniques – '

'Neat!' I said.

'Astral Physics,' he went on, then paused before saying with just the hint of a gulp in his voice, 'and Rocket Mechanics. Your specialist field. That's why I really appreciate the chance of working with you. If you want to find out more about a subject you may as well learn from the best.'

I was liking this guy more and more.

The driver brought the transporter to a halt by the scanner that automatically checked our credentials. A few moments later we were in the tunnel, heading for *Pathfinder*.

We were about halfway along when the transporter juddered suddenly and a few seconds later began to accelerate at alarming speed.

'What's going on, Joe?' I yelled at the driver.

'Steering's gone,' he shouted. 'There's no response whatsoever.'

By now the car was roaring down the tunnel so quickly that the huge mosaic murals on either side depicting major milestones in the colonization of Mars merged into one huge, featureless blur.

'Brake, for Heaven's sake!' My throat hurt in my effort to make myself heard above the roaring engine.

'What do you think I'm trying to do?' Joe boomed.

The veins on Joe's temples bulged as another sudden burst of acceleration pinned Jack and me against our backrests.

Straight ahead I could see an intersection where our tunnel crossed with a larger one used exclusively by nuclear freight tankers.

I looked up. The red warning lights set into the roof of the air lock were flashing on and off, telling us that there was a loaded tanker approaching the crossroads. 'Phew!' I gasped in relief, knowing that a failsafe mechanism built into the roadway would automatically bring our transporter to a stop before we reached the junction.

I braced myself for the moment when the automatic brakes were applied and I would be thrust forward.

It never came.

As we streaked towards the intersection, the huge screen above it suddenly glowed into life, showing an aerial view.

There was our transporter zooming down the tunnel towards the junction.

Thundering down the freight tunnel, getting ever closer to the crossing, was a Grade II Carrier.

And the digital clock at the top of the screen showed impact was ten seconds away.

CHAPTER 4

'Cliché – noun – a word or expression that has lost much of its force through overexposure, as for example "time stood still".'

That's how my dictionary defines the word.

Wrong!

When you are given ten seconds' warning of an impending crash, it is no cliché to say that time stands still. It does. Or at least takes longer to pass than a slow-worm crossing the Sahara Desert.

Nine. Joe's got spots on the back of his neck, I notice.

Eight. Jack's clutching his safety harness so tightly his knuckles are turning blue.

Seven. My back's pressing so hard into the backrest I must be about to go right through it.

Six. I'll never get around to telling Lilo Gruber she's a great big lump of sauerkraut.

Five. My hair's a mess.

Four. Who will Kun ask to investigate Lars Aschengreen's death if I'm not around any more?

Three. My hair's a real mess.

Two. John Meehan, I suppose. Wonder what he'll find.

One. Why am I so obsessed with my hair?

Zero …

Suddenly I was thrown forward so hard that I expected to be wrenched from my harness, shoot over the seat in front of me and crash into the windscreen.

But I wasn't.

I was thrown forward all right. But a nanosecond later it was as if I was floating on a sea of goose down as the air-safety bag in front of me ballooned open and pushed me back into my seat.

'Are you all right, Miss Stravinsky?' I heard Joe say a few seconds later as he wrenched the back door open. I felt him tug me out of my harness and into the tunnel.

'I think so,' I coughed. 'Are you? And Mr Nairn?'

'We're both fine.' Jack's head peeked over the other side of the transporter's roof. 'I thought we were about to crash into the freighter, though. What happened?'

'Second failsafe,' Joe explained. 'Impact-reducing barrier descends if the automatic slowdown malfunctions. Even so I was pretty terrified.'

'Terrified?' Jack giggled nervously. 'I was scared sockless! How's the transporter?'

'Should be OK,' said Joe. 'That new high-tensile steel/rubber alloy is as strong as it comes.'

'And amazingly flexible,' I added.

'What happened?' Jack rubbed his neck as he spoke. 'What made it go out of control?'

'No idea.' Joe shook his head. 'The drive computer must have gone – '

The rest of what he was saying was drowned out by the deafening whine of a siren as a highway security car skidded to a halt beside us.

'You guys all right?' the driver said as the whine faded to a soft purr and then vanished.

'Fine!' I nodded. 'But can you give us a lift, Officer Krupps?' I asked, taking in the name tag on her tunic pocket. 'Please.'

'Where are you going?'

'Bay 6758. That's where my spacecab's parked.'

The officer punched the number into a keyboard on her control panel and a second later I saw my security mugshot fill the screen just above.

'Dianne-Doris Stravinsky! Head of – ' she said,

peering at the screen then turning to look at me. 'Sorry, Miss Stravinsky,' she went on. 'Didn't recognize you. You've grown your hair. Jump in.'

'I'll just get our stuff,' I said, opening the hatch.

'Please!' Jack Nairn sprang forward to help me with my bags. 'I'll take these.'

Clever! Good looking! And nice manners! There's got to be something wrong with this guy, I thought as he took our gear out of the transporter and piled it into the security car.

Then I remembered what it was.

He'd won the Presidential Commendation for Rocket Mechanics at university: I'd only got a gold medal!

'Going far?' Krupps asked as we sped down the rest of the tunnel and into the hangar where my personal jet/rocket-powered spacecab was parked.

'The other side of the *Amazonis Planitia*,' I said.

'Isn't that where Lars Aschengreen and the other guys were killed?' Krupps brought her hand hard down on the horn to get an Agency garbage truck to pull over. 'When their shuttle blew up?'

'Yup!' I said, making a note to report the garbage truck driver for mouthing swearwords at a superior officer.

'Well, I don't know much about the other guys,' sniffed Krupps. 'But as far as Aschengreen's concerned, it couldn't have happened to a nicer guy!'

'Not exactly Mr Popularity, was he?' Jack said as we waved Officer Krupps goodbye and made our way to my spacecab. 'Lars Aschengreen.'

'Next time you're working on screen, call up the dictionary function,' I said. 'Start with abrasive and scroll through every unpleasant adjective till you get to zymotic. Put them together and that's Aschengreen.'

'Zymotic?'

'Relating to an infectious disease!' I grinned. 'Now come on. Let's get going.'

'Your spacecab's just about ready for you, Miss Stravinsky.' Moses Hartley, one of the Agency's top mechanics, saluted as he spoke. 'And all the equipment you asked for has been stowed aboard. You're not using the booster, right?'

'Right, Mo.' I returned his salute. 'It's only a short flight. We're not going into orbit.'

We walked towards the small plane. Alongside the much larger booster it almost looked like a toy.

But this was no plaything. There was enough hydrogen fuel in the inflatable tanks to blow the *Pathfinder* Hangar from here to kingdom come.

Jack was about to clamber into the co-pilot's seat when I stopped him. 'Wanna take her up?'

'Sure!'

'I've got some stuff I've got to catch up on,' I said. 'You do know how to fly this thing, don't you?'

Jack laughed the sort of warm, happy laugh that made you want to join in. 'I've been flying spacecabs since I was at college – before. But don't tell anyone: I was too young to have a licence.'

We climbed into the cockpit and a few minutes later we had taxied out of the hangar and were shooting down the runway at gathering speed. At precisely the right moment Jack pulled down on tilt control to bring the nose up to take-off angle and soon we had left the ground behind.

Call me old fashioned, but to me there's nothing to beat the excitement of a manual take-off. Computer-controlled flight is all very well, but the pilot needs as much skill as a dumb-waiter. With hand controls there's always just the tiniest chance that something may go wrong. And that adds the touch of danger I find so exhilarating.

As we gained height and shot through the pink sky, I relaxed and gazed down at the rusty-red landscape.

The vast plain we were flying over, *Amazonis Planitia*, was pockmarked with craters and criss-crossed with what looked like dried-up river beds.

I remembered reading an old book about these dusty gullies and creeks. All the writers apart from one had agreed that there had never been water on Mars. But one had written, 'If they look like dried-up river beds, have all the features of dried-up river beds, and there's no other explanation for them, maybe they are dried-up river beds!'

He'd been right, of course. Millions of years ago rivers had flowed across the planet.

When I'd told Jack there were things I needed to catch up on, I hadn't been quite honest. What I really wanted to do was to take time out to think about the crash and how Lars Aschengreen's death was going to change things.

No one had said they were sorry he was dead.

People had used expressions like 'a giant among scientists', 'far-sighted genius' and 'brilliant mind', but when I had looked round the table at the Heads of Department meeting, I saw not a shred of regret in anyone's eyes.

In fact, it was almost as if some of them were trying to hide their – pleasure is the wrong word – relief, maybe.

But sorrow?

Not a trace.

CHAPTER 6

I had known Lars Aschengreen since I was a kid. He and Dad had been recruited into the Agency at the same time, as High Fliers, straight from university. They were rivals rather than friends, but Dad had invited him to the house quite often.

I hadn't seen him since Dad quit the Agency to work on his own project. Lots of people believed that Aschengreen should have backed Dad's theory – that by passing nuclear-charged particles through ordinary sea water, it would be possible to extract usable energy. If he had, the Agency would have taken the idea up and pumped money into it.

Instead, Aschengreen had insisted that money would be better spent looking at ways to control the power of earthquakes and volcanoes to provide an answer to the Earth's deepening energy crisis.

The Agency had backed Aschengreen and Dad had resigned to work on his own.

Since then, I hadn't seen Aschengreen until the day I'd arrived on Mars to take up my appointment.

I'd heard about him, though. As Aschengreen's career had blossomed, Dad had become more and more frustrated at the difficulties he was having getting his own ideas accepted. 'I know I'm right, DeeDee,' he'd say when I was old enough to understand. 'If only the Agency had funded me I'd have cracked it by now.'

He was still trying to crack it the day he died.

'All right?' Jack Nairn's voice cut through my thoughts. 'You look as if you're about to cry.'

'I'm fine,' I said. 'Must have something in my eye. How're you doing?'

'No problems,' Jack said. 'This machine handles beautifully. Want to take over? We're about a quarter of the way there.' As he spoke he pulled a small pack from his pocket. 'Gum?'

'No thanks,' I smiled at him. 'To both questions. Carry on. Think I'll try and get some sleep.'

'I thought you had some work you wanted to catch up on.' Jack puckered his nose as he spoke.

'I have been,' I snapped. 'Just because I'm not at a computer doesn't mean I'm not working. Thinking's an important part of any job. You should know that.'

'Pardon me for living,' he said quietly, gazing at me for a moment.

'Sorry!' I said. 'I shouldn't have snapped at you.'

'It's cool,' he said.

'I haven't heard that expression since I was a kid.'

'I don't think I've used it since I was a kid.' His voice sounded relaxed again. 'Now, you said you were going to try to get some sleep.'

'Yup!' I sighed and closed my eyes.

'Since I was a kid.' The words echoed in my head.

Since I was a kid there had been two things I'd wanted. First, for my dad to succeed. Second, to get into the Agency as a High Flier specializing in rocket mechanics.

One out of two isn't bad, I suppose. I may not have seen Dad get what he wanted but I had been recruited as a High Flier and not only had I specialized in rocket mechanics, I was head of the Agency's whole rocket research programme.

I closed my eyes and felt myself drifting off to sleep when I heard Jack's loud gasp.

'What is it?' I cried, coming to immediately.

I looked round. His face was bright red and he was banging his throat with his right hand.

'Jack!' I yelled. 'What is it?'

The only answer I got was a horrible strangulated gurgling and a dreadful rasping.

I'd heard that sound once before: the day Josy Coolidge, a college classmate, had choked on a mouthful of hamburger and almost died.

I looked down and saw a chewing-gum wrapper on Jack's lap. Oh no! He must have gum stuck in his throat.

'Jack!' I tried to keep a note of panic from my voice. Difficult when the pilot has taken both hands from the controls, the spacecab you're travelling in is spiralling out of control and the ground below looks as if it's coming up to meet it!

CHAPTER 7

I knew what to do.

At least I knew what I would have done if we were on the ground and Jack was choking to death. Get behind him, put my arms round him, clasp my hands together and pull them hard against his chest. It's called the Heimlich manoeuvre and it saved Josy's life. One pull and the half-chewed bit of burger had dislodged itself from her throat.

But we weren't on the ground.

We were in a spacecab and Jack was at the controls!

Come on, DeeDee, I said to myself. *Think! There must be something you can do, otherwise it's goodbye world time.*

An idea flashed into my mind.

'Sit hard back in your seat,' I yelled at Jack. 'As hard as you can.'

'What?' Jack croaked, staring at me through his now-bulging eyes as if I was mad.

'Push as hard as you can against your backrest,' I shouted.

I saw him force himself so far back in his seat that I thought for a second he might do it damage.

'This may hurt a little,' I said, trying not to sound like a dentist with a drill in his hand. Then I leaned

over and thumped him hard on his chest, just above
the breast bone.

Nothing!

Outside the world was reeling as the rocky red
Martian surface seem to sink one way then bounce
up the other like a see-saw with springs.

For no reason at all I remembered the day years
ago when a crowd of us from college had gone to a
fortune-teller for a laugh. 'You've got a strong, long life
line,' the old crone had said, peering at my hand.
'You'll live to a good age.'

So much for fortune-telling, I thought, as the
spacecab spiralled ever closer to the ground.

Jack's face was now the colour of a ripe plum.

Once again I leaned over and banged him with all
my might on the same spot.

'Yes!' I yelled, as a blob of gum shot out of his
mouth and slammed into the
cockpit
windscreen.
It hung
there for a
moment before
slithering down
like a pink slug and
dropping to the
floor.

Jack pulled on

the controls to steady the spacecab and as it gained height he turned to me and said, 'Thanks! I owe you one.'

I shrugged my shoulders modestly as if to say, 'Think nothing of it.'

'Where did you learn that?' he went on. 'Boxing classes?'

'It's sort of the Heimlich manoeuvre,' I smiled.

'Sort of?' he said. 'When did you come up with that particular version?'

'About two seconds ago.'

'Wanna take over?'

'May as well,' I said. 'As I don't feel the least bit tired any more.'

Jack switched power over to the controls in front of me and I took the cab up to six thousand metres.

Looming on the horizon was *Olympus Mons*. At around 27,000 metres it was three times higher than Mount Everest with a crater at the top so large it would have held New York City, with enough room left over for most of Tokyo.

'Now that's what I call a mountain.' There was a note of awe in Jack's voice.

'Highest in the solar system, probably,' I said.

Suddenly one of the instruments in front of me started to flash.

'Good,' I smiled. 'It's beaming.'

'The shuttle flight recorder?'

'Yup! Its signal's being picked up by a communication satellite orbiting the planet. We're within range.'

The flashing stopped as suddenly as it had started and what had been a blank screen was now glowing emerald green. As the glow deepened, a line of figures started to appear.

'What's it say?' I asked.

'84°5' north. 36°42' west.'

'Key them in,' I said. 'We may get a visual.'

Jack leaned forward and activated the touch-sensitive screen in front of him. '36°40- what?'

'Two!'

Almost as soon as he had entered the last numbers in, the keyboard vanished and an image of the area the signal was beaming from appeared on the screen.

'Great!' I said through gritted teeth.

'Something tells me you don't mean that,' Jack said.

'It's in the crater!' I sighed. 'At the top of Olympus.'

'What's so awful about that?'

'Olympus is a volcano,' I said. 'That's what's so awful about that!'

CHAPTER 8

'It's extinct, isn't it?' There was a tremor in Jack Nairn's voice.

'Ever heard the expression "The jury's still out on that one"?' I said.

'Yup!' he nodded. 'It means not quite sure, doesn't it?'

'Precisely,' I agreed. 'Olympus hasn't erupted for centuries. But the boffins still haven't decided if it's extinct or not.'

'But surely they must have some way of knowing.' Jack sounded puzzled.

'Ever heard of Mount St Helen's?' I asked.

'In Washington State?' Jack scratched his head. 'Sure. It went off with a bang over a hundred years ago, didn't it? Late 1970s, early 80s?'

'Even though everyone thought it had been extinct for centuries,' I nodded. 'That's the trouble with volcanoes.'

We flew on without speaking for a while, getting closer and closer to the towering mountain.

'How much longer?' Jack broke the silence.

'Few minutes,' I said, checking the instruments in front of me. 'It's quite funny, really.'

'What?'

'That Aschengreen should die on Olympus. Or

above it, rather.'

'Why? Because he was some sort of god and the Greek gods lived on Mount Olympus?'

'Nice try,' I grinned. 'At least it would be if Aschengreen had been some sort of god. He had the vanity, true enough. But he was no god, no matter what he thought of himself.'

'So what's funny?'

'Aschengreen was planning to bombard Olympus with radioactive particles to try to activate a small volcanic explosion,' I said. 'Looks like the mountain got in first.'

'If you think that's funny,' Jack's voice was serious, 'you've got a weird sense of humour.'

'I meant funny peculiar, not funny ha-ha,' I snapped.

By now we were about five kilometres from the huge mountain that blocked the way ahead. 'Hold on to your hat,' I cried. 'I'm taking her up.'

Olympus rose out of the ground at a gentle slope that quickly changed to a steep incline of about sixty degrees. I kept the spacecab about three thousand metres from the craggy surface, shadowing the seemingly endless slope until suddenly we were above the rim of the huge crater at the top.

'Wow!' said Jack, taking in the huge size of what looked like a dull red saucer that stretched as far as the eye could see.

Even I was impressed by the sheer scale of it.

'Millions of years ago Olympus probably had a sharp peak,' I said. 'Ripped off during an explosion, leaving this caldera.'

'Sounds like a Spanish dance, rather than a crater,' Jack smiled. 'Glad I wasn't around when it blew.'

'That makes two of us,' I laughed. 'What's our position?'

'74°15' north, 16°19' west.' Jack peered at the instrument panel.

'Not far to go,' I said. 'Let's take a closer look at the caldera.'

I took the spacecab down until we were skimming so close to the surface we were making the dust rise.

'How big is this crater?' Jack wanted to know.

'Eighty kilometres in dia– '

Before I could finish, Jack shouted, 'There it is. The capsule.'

'It can't be!' I scoffed. 'We're at least twenty

kilometres from the source of the signal.'

'Look for yourself.'

Sure enough. There on the screen, looking like a silver pebble on a rust-coloured beach, was an Agency space capsule. I took the 'cab in close, overshot, and turned so sharply that if I hadn't been strapped in, I'd have landed on Jack's lap.

'There's something not quite right about this,' I shouted, putting the 'cab into such a tight, circular path above the small spacecraft that the engine started to whine in complaint.

'What?' Jack boomed.

'For a High Flier you're remarkably dim,' I said. 'Just think about it.'

Jack frowned for a moment then snapped his fingers and said, 'Of course! If – '

'If Aschengreen's capsule exploded, how come it's down there?' I finished the sentence for him.

'Thanks,' he laughed. 'I was bluffing! For a High Flier you're remarkably easy to fool! I had no idea what you were talking about.'

For a moment I bristled with anger. But when I looked at him the grin on his face was so wide and infectious, I couldn't help laughing along with him. 'Come on. Take over and let's see what's going on.'

Despite a strong wind and having to land on what looked like a badly ploughed field, Jack took the spacecab down and brought her smoothly to a halt about two hundred metres from the spacecraft.

'Nice one,' I complimented him.

'Thanks,' he said as we unbuckled our harnesses and clambered into the pressurized spacesuits hanging on hooks in the small cabin behind.

That's one of the good things about the new generation of spacecabs: they're totally pressurized so you don't have to wear cumbersome spacesuits when you're in one.

But outside? That's a different story.

Suitably dressed, we squeezed into the air lock and a few seconds later we were bounding across the Martian surface like two kangaroos with springs in the soles of their feet. We were helped by the strong wind that caught us from behind and blew us along.

Funny, Mars is my second home now, but I've never quite got used to gravity there. It's slightly less than forty per cent of the Earth's and the slow-motion effect of moving around on the planet is weird.

Every time we landed, our feet sank into a thick layer of red dust, sending up little swirls that caught the wind as we loped across to the capsule.

Even from some distance away I could clearly see the Agency's logo – two doves facing each other across a red globe that symbolized Mars – on the side of the little spaceship.

'It's one of ours.' Jack's voice crackled through my headset.

'It's an escape capsule,' I said.

The same idea must have hit us both at the same moment.

'You mean – ' Jack started, taking a giant stride towards the little spacecraft.

'I wonder if – ' I said, leaping after him, eager to find out if any of the crew had managed to escape.

'It's from Aschengreen's shuttle,' I cried, seeing the letters LA painted under the logo. 'Come on! Help me right it.'

Between us we managed to get the capsule standing on its base.

'How do you open this thing?' Jack panted at the battered metal tube, featureless apart from the logo and a small porthole at head height.

'There's a button on the inside – '

'Fat lot of good that is,' said Jack.

'But from the outside,' I went on, 'it opens by electronic beam.' As I spoke I fumbled in the bag strapped to my waist for a remote control. 'Watch!' I pointed it at the shuttle and pressed a red button.

A pinprick of bright light ran across the shuttle for a moment or two before the automatic search located the receptor. A second later, the outer shell of the tube began to revolve, revealing the entry hatch.

The idea that there could have been a survivor aboard vanished when I saw the capsule was empty. Had I been thinking logically, I should have realized that it would have been. If Aschengreen's capsule had exploded without warning, no one on board would have had time to clamber aboard any of what we called the lifeboats.

I told Jack to inspect the inside, fumbled in my waistbag for my digital camera, and a moment or two later started to snap the capsule from various angles.

As I moved round, the wind was now blowing so strongly I was struggling to keep on my feet.

'One for the family album?' I laughed, catching Jack in my lens as he stood in the hatch, and then seeing the puzzled expression on his face, went on, 'For evidence. That's why I'm taking all these photographs.'

'That's not what I'm puzzled about,' he said. 'I know that every piece of debris from Aschengreen's shuttle we find has to be photographed.'

'So what's bothering you?'

'This,' he said, holding out his arm for me to see what was nestling in the palm of his hand.

'What's puzzling about a piece of red piping?' I said casually.

'It was on the floor.'

'Probably came loose when the mother ship exploded,' I suggested.

'But there's no red pipes in the lifeboat,' Jack said. 'I've checked.'

'Must have come from the mother ship.' I made a face as I spoke.

'But the lifeboat was closed,' Jack persisted. 'You had to open it.'

'In that case it must have been there when the capsule was launched,' I said. 'Maybe fell from a mechanic's pocket or something. Let's see it.'

I took the piece of piping from Jack, peered at it and dropped it into my waistbag.

'Aren't you going to log it as evidence?' Jack asked.

'Of course,' I nodded. 'When we get back to the spacecab. I've just got to take a couple more pictures.'

No sooner had I spoken than I saw the expression on Jack's face change.

He no longer looked puzzled.

He looked absolutely terrified.

CHAPTER 10

'What is it?' I cried.

'Look!' His hand shook slightly as he pointed at something over my shoulder. 'Behind you.'

I spun round as quickly as my awkward spacesuit would allow me. What I saw set my heart hammering against my ribcage so loudly I was surprised Jack couldn't hear its frantic thumping.

What looked like an enormous red pillar with crimson walls on either side was bearing down on us at dizzying speed.

I had never seen a Martian dust storm before. I'd read that a really big one could whip up the surface grit for miles around and carry it for enormous distances, totally changing the shape of the landscape.

I'd seen photographs of flat plains transformed into what looked like storm-bound red seas, their mountainous waves frozen as they towered to their peak.

I'd even heard that in the early days of Martian exploration, a particularly violent sandstorm had covered a large landing craft, trapping the pioneers inside for almost a month before they were rescued.

'The spacecab!' I screamed. 'Quick!'

But it was hopeless.

The wind was howling around us.

'It's no good!' Jack sounded surprisingly calm considering we were now being blown backwards like dandelion clocks caught in a stiff autumn breeze.

'The lifeboat,' I yelled. 'Head for the lifeboat.'

'We don't have much choice,' Jack shouted. 'We're being blown there anyway.'

A second later, I banged hard against it and had to hold on to the side of the entry hatch to stop myself being blown past it.

Despite the gale that was now blowing, I managed to get in.

A second or two later Jack had joined me.

'All right?' I asked.

Jack nodded. 'Much roomier than it looks from the outside,' he said.

'If you press that button by the hatch, it'll close,' I said. 'It will keep the dust out. There's already enough in here to keep a cleaner busy for a week.'

I saw Jack's thumb push hard on the button and

expected to see the outer shell slide over and close the gap to the elements outside.

But nothing happened.

Instead, all I saw was the wall of red dust getting closer and closer.

'The dust must be jamming the mechanism,' Jack yelled.

I was about to try to squeeze past him and peer outside when suddenly the wind gusted so violently that he was thrown off balance. 'Look out!' I cried as he crashed into me and knocked me against the wall behind.

'What's happening?' he shouted as the shuttle shuddered for a moment, then swung back to an alarming angle, and teetered for a second before crashing over.

As it fell it must have spun round for now the open hatch was facing away from the heap of dust.

'Thank goodness for that,' I spluttered. 'At least the dust won't get in now. We can shelter here till it blows over.'

But no sooner had I spoken than the shuttle started to roll over and over like a barrel.

'What's happening?' Jack shouted.

'We must be in the eye of the storm,' I yelled.

I don't know how long we were thrown this way and that before the capsule came to a halt.

'OK, DeeDee?' he asked.

'I'm all right,' I said. 'You?'

'No bones broken, at any rate,' he replied. 'Let's get out of this thing.'

I looked around.

This, I thought to myself, *is just not your day, DeeDee old girl.*

'Jack,' I said weakly. 'I think we're trapped.'

'Trapped!' The word shot from his mouth. 'What do you mean, trapped?'

'We've come to a standstill hatch down.'

Jack's gulp echoed in my headset. 'You mean – '

'I mean the hatch is blocked. Goodness knows how many metres of dust there are beneath us. How are we going to get out?'

'Dig?' Jack suggested. 'Like moles?'

I shook my head. 'In these suits we couldn't dig our way through candy floss!'

'Mayday bleeper?'

'By the time anyone could get here our air supplies will have run out.'

'Prayer!'

I didn't know if Jack was joking or not.

'I think I've got an idea,' Jack went on before I got back to him on the subject of prayer. 'If we both lie on our backs across the capsule, and rock backwards and forwards, maybe we could roll it over.'

'What about the packs on our backs?'

'Let's just hope they'll be strong enough to take

the weight,' Jack said. 'Come on! Any better ideas?'

I shook my head. 'OK,' I said. 'Let's give it a whirl.'

We both lay down, our bodies parallel to the bottom of the hatch.

'On three,' Jack said. 'One. Two. Three!'

We rocked backwards and forwards in almost perfect time with each other.

'It's moving!' Jack cried. 'Harder!'

'Yes!' I yelled as the capsule began to roll over. A second or two later I could see the pink Martian sky overhead as the spacecraft came to a stop after it had turned 180 degrees.

'Gently does it,' I said, slowly getting to my feet. 'We don't want it to do the full circle.'

A few moments later we were out of the capsule, standing knee-deep in the rust-coloured dust. 'Let's get out of here,' Jack said. 'Let's get to where the signal was coming from.'

'I just hope the wind blew itself out before it got there.' I flicked some dust from my shoulder.

'It already has,' Jack said, looking around. 'It's not even stirring the dust now. Come on, let's get back to the – ' He stopped dead in his tracks. 'Oh, no!' He sounded as if there were tears in his voice. 'The spacecab! It's vanished!'

Looking around, I felt as if I had been dropped in the middle of a vast red desert.

Through the visor of his helmet, I saw Jack staring hopelessly around him.

'Don't panic,' I said, once again fumbling in my waistbag, this time for the small sensor tuned in to the spacecab's automatic guidance system.

As soon as I had activated it, I held it at arm's length and turned slowly around, waiting for the bleeps it was sending out to merge into a continuous whine. Then it would be pointing in the right direction.

'Over there,' I said. 'Somewhere!'

As we walked away from the lifeboat, the signal got stronger and stronger, until we had gone about two hundred metres when it started to fade slightly.

I stepped back and the whine reached its peak again. 'We're standing on top of it,' I tried to sound matter-of-fact. 'Come on. Let's get digging.'

'How come the storm covered the 'cab but not the lifeboat?' Jack asked.

I shrugged my shoulders and shook my head. 'Dunno,' I said. 'You never can tell with dust storms.'

We knelt down and began to scoop handfuls of dust from the ground. Sure enough, within less than a minute, we had uncovered the top of the cockpit.

'This is going to take forever,' Jack sighed.

'Hang on,' I said, getting to my feet. 'There's a shovel in the lifeboat. I'll get it.'

'I'll come with you,' Jack volunteered.

'Scared the little green men will get you if I leave you on your own?' I joked.

'No!' Jack sounded annoyed. 'To stop the lifeboat rolling over when you're inside it.'

A few minutes later we were back beside the partially unearthed spacecab, taking it in turns to throw great spadefuls of dust into the thin Martian atmosphere.

'That should do it,' I said when we had uncovered the entry hatch. 'The dust is so fine, if we switch to vertical take-off, we should break free.'

We clambered into the cockpit and switched on the engine. For a second the spacecab shuddered like a skeleton with the shakes, but then in an enormous cloud of dust we rose slowly straight upwards until we were about twenty metres off the ground.

'Take her away,' I said.

Jack re-angled the thrust directors. The moment he did so, the spacecab hovered where it was for a second before the nose tilted upwards to forty degrees and we shot forwards so quickly that I felt as if someone was pushing me into my backrest.

There was no sign of the dust storm and we flew

smoothly on to where our instruments told us we would find Aschengreen's flight recorder.

When we were about five kilometres away one of the cameras scanning the ground focused on a large piece of metal.

'Reduce speed!' I ordered and put the camera into close-up mode.

'There's part of the outer shell. Thank goodness the dust storm blew itself out before it got here,' I said. 'Take the cab up to ten thousand metres and hover there.'

As we soared higher and higher the cameras picked out more and more debris from Aschengreen's capsule. Gradually a definite pattern began to emerge.

'I'd say it exploded when it was at true vertical.'

'How can you tell?' Jack asked.

'The debris is scattered in more or less a circle,' I explained. 'If it was flying at an angle we'd be looking at an egg shape.'

'Won't the flight recorder tell us that?'

'They can malfunction, especially if there's been a violent explosion,' I said. 'And judging from the spread of the wreckage I'd say it was a violent explosion.'

I gazed at the screens for a moment or two more before telling Jack to take the spacecab down and land it at 85°5' north, 36°42' west.

'What are we looking for?' he asked when we were out of the cab.

'A square black box about the size of a laptop.'

'Like that one over there?' Jack pointed to a cluster of debris a few metres away. 'By that coil of wires.'

'Well spotted!' I cried, bouncing towards it. 'I didn't expect to find it quite so quickly.'

'All part of the service,' Jack laughed.

'Give me a hand, please,' I asked. 'It's jammed between some rocks.'

Jack got down on his knees, gripped the edge sticking out of the ground, and tugged as hard as he could. 'No good,' he panted. 'I don't suppose you've got a hammer and chisel in that waistbag of yours?'

'No, they're in the spacecab,' I said. 'I'll go and fetch them.'

I started to go back to the 'cab but a second later I heard a loud crackle from behind. 'Jack!' I cried, turning round. 'What's wrong?'

But even as I spoke, he slumped, twitching, to the ground.

CHAPTER 12

As quickly as I could I bounded towards him. The moment I was by his side I saw the wires in his hand.

I brought my rubber-soled boot down hard on them, twisting them out of his grip. Instantly he stopped twitching and a few seconds later was struggling to get to his feet.

'What happened?' I asked, helping him.

'I went to clear the wires,' he said shakily, 'but as soon as I touched them — big-time shock.'

'The wires can't be live,' I said, shaking my head. 'It's barely possible.'

'You hold them then.'

'No way!' My eye followed the line of cables that wound its way from where we were standing to behind a rock a few metres away. 'Let's go and see.'

'I don't believe it,' Jack gasped a few moments later when we were on the far side of the rock, staring at a half-shattered solar-powered battery, wires spilling from it in all directions. 'It's still working.'

'Just!' I said.

'Just enough to bring me to my knees,' said Jack. 'Come on. Let's get that flight recorder. And then we'll unload the buggy and cover as much of the area as we can.'

We spent the next few hours roaming all over

the place, Jack driving, me looking for debris. We packed small pieces into the buggy's storage boxes and attached electronic tags to the larger bits so that they could still be located if they became covered by dust before the Agency's recovery men were sent to carry them back to base.

The largest thing we found was an almost complete section of the crew compartment, standing upright behind a huge boulder.

'You don't suppose – ' Jack gulped.

'I shouldn't think so,' I said, answering his unspoken question. 'Judging from the way the debris is scattered, the capsule went up with quite a bang. Everyone on board would be – '

'Blown to bits?'

'Very small bits,' I whispered sadly. 'They wouldn't know a thing about it. It would be over in – ' I was about to say 'a flash' but it was hardly appropriate in the circumstances – 'in an instant.'

We stood in silence for a moment, both picturing the scene aboard the capsule before the explosion. People in Flight Control I had talked to back at base had confirmed Aschengreen had been at the helm when it had taken off from there to prepare the target area on *Olympus Mons*.

Had he still been in the pilot's seat when it had left the mountain aiming for Deimos? The voice recorder we'd found would tell us that.

Just another routine take-off. And then at around ten thousand metres ...

No time for any last words.

No goodbyes.

Just a sudden bang that killed everyone on board before they even knew what had happened.

'Poor guys,' Jack sighed.

'Yup!' I looked away from the wreckage. 'Come on, let's get on with it while it's still light. You cover that area over there. I'll search around that rock straight ahead.'

As I made my way towards it, I started to wish that I could feel something for Aschengreen. He had no family to grieve for him. His wife had left him a long time ago, fed up with playing tenth fiddle to his career, and I'd heard that his daughter had been killed in a car crash.

No one I knew liked him.

Respected him? Yes.

Admired his work? Certainly.

But liked him? No one.

I was almost at the rock when I spotted another piece of debris that looked interesting, but just as I knelt to examine it more closely Jack's voice came through my headset. 'DeeDee,' he said. 'Is that bit of metal I found in the lifeboat still in your waistbag?'

'I guess so,' I said. 'Why?'

'I think you'd better come over here.'

He was leaning over a bit of debris I recognized right away.

'That's part of the fuel system,' I said.

'That's what I thought,' said Jack. 'And see there,' he went on, pointing at a gap in it.

'So it was damaged by the explosion?' I said in a so-what sort of voice. 'Surprising if it hadn't been.'

'Can I see that piece of metal?'

'Sure!' I said, reaching into my waistbag for it.

'Thought so.' There was a note of triumph in Jack's voice. 'Exactly the same shade of red as the pipe. And look.' As he spoke he pushed it into the gap in the pipe. 'There. A perfect fit.'

'What are you getting at, Jack?' I asked, furrowing my brow.

'The pipe was cut deliberately,' he said quietly. 'Aschengreen and the others didn't die in an accident. They were murdered.'

CHAPTER 13

'Are you sure, Stravinsky?'

It was the following day, after Jack and I had returned from Olympus and I was making my preliminary report to my senior colleagues.

'Certain, sir.' I highlighted the fuel system on the graphic of the doomed capsule's internal structure that filled the large screen in Jiri Kun's office. 'Watch! The flight recorder confirms that this is what happened. I checked it myself and programmed this simulation.'

I keyed in the necessary commands and every eye in the room watched the ignition sequence get underway. On one of the screens to the right of the main one, we saw the capsule rise off the ground.

At five thousand metres fuel surged through the damaged pipe.

At seven thousand metres, it spilled through the cut.

At eight thousand it ignited and a split second later, when the capsule had gained another two thousand metres, there was a bright flash and it shattered into countless pieces that drifted down to the surface like snowflakes caught in a gentle breeze.

'Could you run us through events?' It was Lilo Gruber who broke the silence. 'From the beginning.'

'Of course,' I nodded. 'As we know, Lars Aschengreen was convinced that there must be a way of harnessing the power of natural phenomena. Earthquakes and volcanoes mainly. He'd been working on his theory for years.'

'Without getting anywhere,' muttered Bill Tuckett, Head of Finance.

'Perhaps not,' snapped Lilo. 'But he was on the verge of success. Or so he said in that last paper he read to us at the February meeting.'

* * * * *

I remembered that meeting.

It was one of the most ill-tempered I had ever attended.

Lars had gone over a lot of old ground and some new territory before seeking our approval for his latest experiment.

'You mean you are deliberately going to try to cause an eruption on *Olympus Mons?*' Matz Borlin had been amazed.

'Not one. Several,' Aschengreen had answered. 'To prove my theory that the power released by a small, controlled eruption can be used to set up a chain reaction of smaller ones. If it works on Mars, there's no reason why it shouldn't work on Earth and provide an energy source that will last for centuries – '

'That's what they said about solar power at the end of the last century and look what happened to that idea,' Charles Lisner interrupted. 'It went out the window with the atmospheric changes global warming caused. And anyway you can't store volcanic power, never mind control it.'

'My experiments in the laboratory show that it can be controlled,' snapped Aschengreen. 'And if we can control it we can generate electricity from it.'

'If you're so certain,' Charles's voice was rising, 'how come no government on Earth will give the Agency permission to put your theories into practice?'

The look Aschengreen had shot Charles was pure poison.

Things had gone downhill from then on. Aschengreen was constantly interrupted by his increasingly hostile heads of department when he told them his plans to lead a four-man team to Deimos, the farther of the two moons orbiting Mars.

From there he planned to bombard low-impulse nuclear particles onto a trigger mechanism on Olympus Mons. This, he was certain, would cause a small eruption. 'But when the particle beam is switched off, the eruption will cease!'

Tempers had frayed and then snapped. Words like 'madness', 'sheer stupidity', 'irresponsible' and 'terrifying consequences' had flown round the room along with others that would have made a sailor blush.

'How do you know you can contain it to a small eruption?' Matz Borlin had asked.

'Computer analyses and forecasts confirm my opinion,' Aschengreen had replied.

'Computers aren't infallible,' Andrew Saunders, Head of Mining Operations, joined in the argument. 'They're only as good as the people operating them.'

'And if anything goes wrong with the nuclear particle beam you could blow the planet to bits if Olympus really lets fly,' Graham Payne, Chief Surveyor objected.

'Or send up a radioactive cloud that would linger in the atmosphere here for years,' Frederic Mann, Number One at Human Resources said before Aschengreen could respond to Graham's ominous objection.

'Why Deimos and not Phobos?' asked Prudence Bismark who ran the Agency's IT systems. 'It's half the distance away. Less!'

Aschengreen explained that he needed to focus the beam on Olympus for four hours. Phobos orbited Mars once every seven-and-a-bit hours. 'That doesn't give me long enough,' he said. 'Deimos takes more than thirty hours. That gives me plenty of time.'

The meeting had broken up after Aschengreen had bullied everyone into submission and left the room with a smug expression on his face.

* * * * *

'I think we all remember that meeting,' Jiri Kun said, looking around the table. 'It was deeply unpleasant.'

'Who was it who said we had to do something to stop Aschengreen?' Lilo looked round the table. 'Someone did, after he left the room. Can't remember who, though.'

'Me!' Matz Borlin half-raised a hand. 'I was just saying what we all felt, wasn't I?'

I think every head around the table nodded.

'That doesn't mean we wanted him dead,' murmured Matz.

I looked slowly from face to face before taking a deep breath and saying, 'Well, somebody did.'

'And whoever that person is,' Jiri Kun said, looking at me, 'is precisely what Headquarters on Earth would like you to find out, Stravinsky.'

'Me?' I think I sounded absolutely thunderstruck. 'But you're Head of Security, Kun.'

Jiri nodded. 'I know. But Headquarters believe you have the sharpest brain of any of us here and are best qualified to find out who the killer is.'

The look that Lilo Gruber shot at me would have made a vampire vomit. The others looked down at the desks in front of them, stared into space or gazed at the graphic of the Aschengreen shuttle glowing on the screen. They were looking anywhere but at me.

'I don't suppose I have any say in the matter?' I said.

Jiri shook his head. 'Orders are orders,' he murmured.

'OK,' I said. 'If that's what they want.'

I gazed at Lilo who was still staring at me, a venomous look glittering in her eyes. 'I'll need to know who had access to the capsule between the last time it was used and when Aschengreen took it out,' I said to her.

'It's on record,'

she said. 'On my computer files.'

'You'll need to give me your security password.' My lips curled into a sickly sweet smile.

I saw her glance quickly at Jiri who nodded so slightly I almost didn't notice.

'Of course,' she returned my smile, double sweet.

'And I'll need to see your files on all employees here on Mars,' I turned to Frederic Mann.

'Whatever for?' He sounded taken aback by my request.

'Because whoever killed Aschengreen must have had a motive, and there may be something in someone's file to give me a clue.'

'There are hundreds of us here,' Frederic said.

'I know.' I turned my gaze on Jiri. 'That's why I'd like an assistant.'

'Who?'

'Jack Nairn,' I said. 'He's a smart guy. He impressed me.'

'Very well.'

I heard Matz Borlin clear his throat.

'Yes, Matz?' Jiri said. 'You want to say something?'

'Something has just struck me,' he said in his slightly stilted English. 'Well, two things, really.'

'Go on,' said Jiri encouragingly.

'First, the escape capsule or lifeboat?' He looked at me as if he was looking for confirmation that he had used the expression correctly.

I nodded back. 'What about it?'

'How is it that it survived the explosion intact?'

That had worried me too. 'When we got back I heard from mission control that Aschengreen had contacted them after he landed on Olympus,' I said. 'He told them that the equipment he was taking to Deimos was heavier than expected and had caused a slight problem on the first leg of the journey. Said he was going to leave one of the lifeboats behind. There was still one to spare.'

'Thanks,' Matz said.

'What's the second thing?' I asked.

Matz looked at each of us in turn and then said: 'We are all assuming that Aschengreen was the intended victim.'

'You mean – ?' Jiri began.

'It could have been one of the other three?' Charles finished the sentence for him.

'If that's the case,' Matz said, 'you could be looking for a murderer but have no idea who his or her intended victim was!'

'Poor DeeDee.' Lilo may have still been smiling, but she sounded about as sympathetic as a judge about to pass the death sentence. 'I think I'd rather look for a needle in a haystack. At least I'd know where the haystack was!'

I'm going to wipe that smile off that lump of lard's face, I thought to myself before snapping my fingers and saying, 'Silly cow.'

'I beg your pardon!' Lilo's jaw dropped. 'How dare you!'

'Not you, Lilo,' I said sweetly. 'Me. I won't be needing your password after all.'

'But how will you know who could have sabotaged the shuttle?' She narrowed her eyes and stared at me suspiciously as she spoke.

'Well, assuming it wasn't Aschengreen on a suicide mission, it could only have been one of three.'

'Who?' four voices chorused.

'One of the other crew,' I said. 'The craft got to Olympus Mons safely, didn't it?'

Several heads nodded.

'So it stands to reason that the fuel pipe was cut after it landed there, before it took off for the second time en route for Deimos.'

'But if you're right,' said Jiri, 'whoever cut the pipe must have known he would die when the shuttle went bang.'

'Assuming he was on board,' someone, I think it was Matz, said.

'Must have been.' I drummed the fingers of my

right hand on the table as I spoke. 'If he wasn't, where is he now? Wandering around the caldera on the top of Olympus Mons? Hiding somewhere?' I shook my head. 'No! He was one of the crew all right.'

'But which one?' Lilo stared at me.

'Let's just hope there's something in Human Resources' files to give us a clue.' I turned to Frederic Mann. 'Can we have a look right away?'

'Sure,' he nodded. 'Let's go to my office.'

* * * * *

I know my office wasn't exactly tidy, but compared to Frederic Mann's it was a tip.

My desk is littered with debris. His was empty apart from a pencil-slim screen opposite the chair.

I've got papers spilling out of drawers, piled on the floor, pinned to the wall – everywhere. There wasn't one to be seen anywhere in Frederic's office.

The books on my shelves were spine-in, spine-out, upright, on their sides, rammed in any old how. His were so neatly lined up they looked as if they had been painted on the walls.

He downloaded the personnel files of the four men who had been on the doomed shuttle onto my micro and gave it back to me. 'There you are,' he said. 'I've security-cleared them for you.'

'Thanks,' I said. 'I'll let you have them back when

I'm through with them.'

'No need,' he smiled. 'Delete them.'

* * * * *

Jack was sitting on the floor of my office, legs crossed, eyes closed, hands resting on his knees.

'Snap out of it,' I said, closing the door. 'Work to do.'

'You should try it,' he said, opening his right eye very slowly and making a face at me. 'It'll make you less tense.'

'Listen, kid,' I snarled at him, 'I was doing yoga when you were a baby. And who said I was tense?'

'You're as tense as a tightrope that's about to snap,' he yawned, getting to his feet. 'What's that you've got there?'

'Never seen a micro before?' I said. 'Come on, we've got work to do.'

'What?'

As I copied the files from my micro-computer onto his mini-laptop, I explained that the Agency had asked me to investigate what was now being called 'The Aschengreen Incident', and how the killer had to be one of three men.

'Let's just hope there's something in these files that tells us which one,' I said. 'Get reading.'

I don't know how long we sat there, scrolling

through page after page, before I heard Jack's sharp intake of breath. 'Got something?' I asked.

'Could be. Take a look at Dr Cooper's file. Page 5.'

'Simon Cooper?'

'Yup.'

I input C-O-O-P-E-R, pressed the Find key, and read the first three pages. 'Don't see anything.'

'Run Aschengreen's file on a sub-screen. Early career details in the Agency.'

'Hang on!' I said. 'Right. With you!'

'See what I mean?' Jack asked.

'Yes!' I said. 'He was appointed to three divisions in his early days with the Agency and each time Aschengreen followed him in and was promoted over him. Enough to make anyone jealous. Wonder if he kept a diary.'

'It'd make interesting reading if he did,' Jack mused.

'There's only one way to find out,' I said. 'Come on.'

Jack followed me out of my office and a few minutes later we were in Simon Cooper's quarters. 'Now where would he keep his diary,' I wondered, looking around, 'if he did keep one?'

'He worked in Computer Systems, didn't he?' Jack said.

I nodded. 'He was brilliant. He programmed the

Deimos experiment.'

'Probably on disk then.'

I sat behind Cooper's desk, tugging at the drawers.

'Locked?' Jack looked quizzically at me.

'So?' I said, picking up a silver paper knife from the desktop. I slid the tip into each lock, opening all the drawers in turn.

'What's this?' I said, taking a large metal box marked PRIVATE AND CONFIDENTIAL from the bottom drawer.

Again, the paper knife made short work of the lock. 'This could be what we're looking for,' I said when I saw the rows of neatly labelled disks inside. 'There's a disk for every year from 2075 right up to now.'

'They're sure to be snoop-proof,' Jack said.

'Come on, Jack,' I smiled. 'You and I both know there's no such thing. And if you can't access these disks, then you're not the High Flier I take you to be.'

'Your office or mine?' Jack grinned.

* * * * *

'Wow!' Jack sat back in his chair. 'I've never read anything so full of hate as this before. He loathed Aschengreen.'

'That's putting it mildly,' I said. 'Mind you, if what he writes is true, it's hardly surprising.'

'About Aschengreen stealing Cooper's ideas?'

'Over and over again,' I nodded. 'No wonder he said he'd like to kill him given half a chance.'

'But that was all years ago,' Jack mused. 'Imagine waiting all this time to get revenge.'

'I think I can understand that,' I said. 'Ever heard the expression "Revenge is a dish best enjoyed cold"?'

'Meaning?'

'The longer you wait, the better it is.' I shrugged my shoulders before going on, 'I think we've got our man.'

CHAPTER 16

'You are quite certain it was Simon Cooper?' Jiri Kun stared at me.

'He had the motive and the opportun– '

'Even if it meant dying himself,' Lilo Gruber interrupted me.

'I was coming to that.' I glared at the old crone. 'Cooper was terminally ill. He found out six months ago, according to his diary.'

'How long did he have left to live?' Frederic Mann sounded puzzled.

'A few months at the most,' I said. 'According to what he wrote his doctor told him.'

'Was this is in his records, Dr Mann?' Jiri's voice hardened.

'No,' Frederic said. 'But it should have been. If it had he'd have been sent back to Earth.' He turned and looked at me. 'Who's his doctor?'

'Rob Snashall,' I said.

'I think we need to talk to him.' Jiri leaned forward, flicking one of the switches on the intercom in front of him. 'Ask Dr Snashall to come to my office,' he said to the secretary who answered. 'Right away.'

While we waited for him to appear, I circulated extracts from Cooper's diaries. 'Look at the entry for

20 March, 2087,' I said.

'*One day someone will kill him. Probably me,*' Matz Borlin read aloud.

'There's much more in the same vein,' I said.

'I don't think I need much more convincing,' Jiri said a few moments later.

'Nor me,' added Matz.

'Great,' I smiled, greatly relieved. 'I can get on with my own work now.'

'Well done, Stravinsky,' Jiri congratulated me. 'And thank you.'

There was a chorus of 'Hear, hear' and 'Nice one, DeeDee' from everyone; well, everyone apart from one and there's no prizes for guessing who that was.

'Thanks,' I said. 'But it's really Jack Nairn who deserves most of the credit.'

'I'm sure you'll write that in your rep–, ' Jiri's last word was drowned out by a confident knock on the door. 'Come in!' he called.

I liked the young American who stepped into the room. He was a popular member of staff, and not just because he was a good doctor. He was a talented pianist and singer, who often entertained us when we were off-duty with songs from twentieth-century musicals.

'Good afternoon.' He was smiling as usual. 'You wanted me, sir?'

'Yes, Doctor. Sit down, please.' Jiri pointed to the

empty seat Aschengreen would have been sitting in had he still been alive.

Jiri came straight to the point. 'Simon Cooper was one of your patients, wasn't he?'

Rob nodded as the smile faded from his face to be replaced by a sad expression.

'Why was the fact that he was terminally ill not noted in his personnel records?'

'But it was.' Snashall looked astonished. 'It's standard procedure.'

'Sorry to have to contradict you, Doctor,' said Frederic Mann. 'There's no mention of it.'

'But there must be.' Snashall held Frederic's stare. 'After every consultation, I wrote up his notes and c-mailed a copy to your in-tray. I must say I was surprised that he was allowed to remain active. I thought he'd have been sent home to enjoy what little time he had left.'

All eyes were on Frederic. 'There was nothing,' he murmured. 'Ever.'

'OK,' I said. 'If Rob says he c-mailed Frederic about Cooper, and Frederic never got them, they must have been either deleted before he had a chance to download them, or they were diverted to another terminal.'

'How?' said Lilo Gruber.

'Cooper was a computer whizzkid,' I said.

'Hardly a kid,' said Lilo. 'He was over forty.'

'Thank you, Lilo,' I said through gritted teeth. 'When do you write up your notes, Rob?'

'Immediately after each consultation,' Rob answered. 'And if anyone else has to be informed, I c-mail their in-trays immediately.'

'Did Simon know this?'

Snashall nodded. 'Yes,' he said. 'I remember the first time he came to see me. I think he knew how ill he was, even then. I explained my routine to him when he was putting his shirt back on. I remember telling him that because he was so senior I'd have to send my notes direct to Dr Mann and not one of his assistants. First time I'd had to do that. In fact the only time. I remember telling Cooper that too.'

'Was he still there when you c-mailed Mann?'

'Yes! In fact he showed me a short cut.'

'What sort of short cut?' Lilo Gruber asked.

'He did something to my speed-dial system.' Rob shrugged his shoulders. 'Don't know what, he was the computer buff.' He paused and looked round the table. 'You know how when you speed-dial a c-mail it usually takes a second or two to connect?'

I think we all nodded.

'Well, after Cooper had done whatever it was he did, there was no delay whatsoever.'

'Can I access Dr Snashall's computer memory via your system, Jiri?' I asked.

He nodded.

I moved to his computer and keyed in the
commands he dictated. Once I was in Rob's system I
brought up his speed-dial directory.

'What's your c-mail number, Frederic?' I said
without taking my eyes from the screen.

'FMHR1!'

'That's it then,' I said a few moments later after I
had checked the directory. 'Cooper changed it so that
whenever Rob speed-dialled Frederic about his
illness, the c-mail went to his own terminal. There's
no way Rob would have known unless he'd run a
directory check.'

'Never crossed my mind,' Rob said.

'Why should it?' Jiri smiled sympathetically at the
doctor.

'So shall I sum up?' I said as I returned to my seat at the table. 'Simon had a long-term grudge against Lars Aschengreen. It smouldered for years and when he found out his days were numbered, he decided it was time for revenge. He had nothing to lose after all. So he flew to *Olympus Mons* with Aschengreen and the other two and when he had a chance to, cut the fuel pipe.'

'Cut?' Rob Snashall sounded surprised.
'What with?'

'A small metal hacksaw, judging from the marks on the piece of pipe we found in the lifeboat,' I said. 'Why?'

'In that case, Simon Cooper couldn't possibly have done it.'

'We were wrong,' I said as I walked through Jiri's outer office where Jack was at his screen. 'Come on, we're back where we started.'

'What!' he sighed. 'You mean it wasn't Cooper?'

I shook my head. 'Nope! Apparently he was suffering from a muscle-wasting disease. According to the doctor, he couldn't have gripped a saw hard enough to cut through a metal pipe.'

'But – '

'No buts. Come on.'

As we walked down the corridor that led to my office, a young man came out of another office and almost banged into us. 'Sorry, Jack,' he said and then gulped when he saw who Jack was with. 'Miss St-st-stravinsky,' he stammered. 'S-s-s-orry, I should have been looking where I was g-g-g-oing.'

'That's all right, Marc.' I liked the blushing young Frenchman. It was hard not to. Not only was he movie-star good looking with shining black hair that flopped over his brow, and coal-black eyes to match, he was unbelievably charming, unbelievably clever and unbelievably modest. Even Lilo Gruber softened whenever he was around.

'Still on for tennis tonight?' he said to Jack.

'If I'm allowed out,' Jack nodded at me.

'What time?' I asked.

'I've booked a court for eight,' Marc said.

'I'll make sure he's there,' I smiled. 'You know what they say about all work and no play.'

Jack and I spent the rest of the afternoon and early evening painstakingly going through the records of the other two men who had died with Aschengreen. And what did we come up with? Absolutely nothing. No old scores to settle. Zilch!

'OK. That's enough for tonight,' I said, glancing at my watch. 'It's a quarter to eight. You're due on the tennis court in fifteen minutes. Mind if I watch?'

'Nope!' Jack shrugged his shoulders. 'Didn't have you down as a sports fan, though.'

I'm not, I thought, *but Marc Desmoulins looks great in tennis gear.*

* * * * *

He didn't only look good. He was good.

So was Jack. They'd obviously played together a lot before because Jack was quite at ease against a left-hander, something that many right-handed players find difficult.

I'd watched them for about half an hour before deciding to call it a day, but waited until they were taking a break at the end of the first set before standing up and shouting 'goodnight'.

'Blast!' I heard Marc cry as I made to leave the courtside. 'The binding on my grip's going, and I've left the tape in my quarters,' he said.

'It's all right,' I said. 'I pass your quarters on the way to mine. If you tell me where it is, I'll have one of the couriers bring it to you. Keep the sweat going.'

'Thanks, Miss Stravinsky,' he said, rummaging in his bag and taking out his smart card. 'That'll get you in. The tape's on the table in my living area, I think.'

'I'll send this back with the tape,' I said, taking the card.

The roll of binding tape was just where Marc had said it was. I picked it up and looked around for his communication system so I could call a messenger.

The system was set in the wall just above a shelf.

I reached for the remote control and was just about to press the button when I noticed a framed photograph on the shelf.

The likeness was unmistakable.

What, I asked myself, was Marc Desmoulins doing with a photograph of Lars Aschengreen's dead daughter in his room?

CHAPTER 18

'OK, Marc,' I said. 'Tell everyone what you told me last night.'

It was the next morning and we were back in Jiri Kun's office.

Marc pushed the thick black hair off his forehead. 'Her name was Lara Dowell. We met at college. She was pretty, clever and fun to be with. Bubbly. Always laughing. Great company.'

He paused for a moment, smiling softly to himself.

'We started dating and pretty soon it started to get serious,' he went on. 'She took me down to Virginia to meet her parents, Dr and Mrs Dowell, and I took her to France to meet mine. We went skiing. Had a wonderful time.'

Again he paused, but this time the smile in his eyes had been replaced by tears that made his eyes glitter like black diamonds.

No one spoke.

'My parents adored her.' Again the smile. 'Everyone did. I remember when we were at the airport waiting for our flight back to the States, my dad joked that Mum was already planning what to wear at the wedding!

'We were too young to get married, we both

knew that. We were still at college and we both wanted to get our careers off the ground before settling down. But we decided to get engaged. And it was only then she told me that Dr Dowell was her step-father. Her real father was Lars Aschengreen. Her mother had divorced him when Lara was a baby and she thought of Dowell as her father. She'd even taken his name. But – '

His voice started to shake.

'But what?' Lilo said softly after a moment or two.

Marc cleared his throat. 'But', he went on, 'when we told the Dowells we were engaged – we drove down to Virginia to tell them, rather than c-mail or phone them – Mrs Dowell said we'd have to ask Aschengreen.'

'Why?' Jiri asked.

'Something to do with the divorce settlement,' Marc replied. 'Apparently Aschengreen had agreed to pay Lara's school and college fees on condition that she spent part of her vacation each year with him. That, and she had to ask his permission before getting engaged. If she went against his wishes and married someone he disapproved of, all the money he had spent on her would have to be repaid.'

'What on earth was he up to?' Frederic Mann wondered.

'I think I can answer that,' Jiri said. 'Lars was a

proud, vain man. So vain that he wouldn't want his only child to marry someone he considered inferior. His grandchildren might not be going to bear his name, but he would do everything he could to ensure they had first-class brains.'

'One hundred per cent right,' Marc nodded. 'Lara took me to Aschengreen's apartment to introduce us. It was clear from the start that there was no way he considered me smart enough to marry his daughter.

'I went for a walk while she pleaded with him but it was no good. He wouldn't change his mind. We went back to college and worked out how much we'd have to pay him if we went against his wishes.'

'Lots, I expect,' murmured Lilo.

'More than lots,' said Marc. 'Lara had been to the best schools. And her college fees alone would have kept a family of five. There was no way we could raise an amount like that. And the Dowells aren't rich. Even if they were, they've got other kids.

'Anyway, once we'd worked out we couldn't repay Aschengreen, Lara decided to go and see him again. To plead with him. Beg him. And if he still said no, she said she was going to tell him we were going to get married eventually and he would have to sue to get his money.

'She was halfway there when – when –' Marc sounded as if he was about to cry.

'It's all right,' said Lilo. 'Take your time.'

'She was behind a truck. One of its tyres burst and it jack-knifed. She was only doing fifty-five. But she didn't stand a chance. Her car slammed into it and bounced  across the highway straight into the path of another truck. It sliced the car in two.'

The tears were running down his cheeks now. 'It was all Aschengreen's fault. If he'd given us permission to get engaged, she wouldn't have been there. She would still be alive. I'm glad he's dead. Really glad. But I didn't kill him.' He looked at each of us in turn. 'You've got to believe me. I didn't kill him.'

'Calm down,' Jiri said. 'Go back to your quarters and stay there until we need to speak to you again. OK?'

Marc nodded and we all watched as he left the room.

'He certainly had the motive,' said Jiri.

'And the opportunity,' added Lilo. 'I've checked everyone's work sheets. Everyone who had access to Aschengreen's shuttle before he set off for *Olympus Mons*. Desmoulins was the last man to sign off from the final maintenance check. He had more than enough time to cut through a fuel pipe.'

'But the pipe wasn't cut until the ship was on Olympus!' said Frederic Mann.

Just then my bleeper went.

'I told you I wasn't to be disturbed,' I snapped, once I had activated it. 'This had better be good.'

I listened to what Jack had to say then switched it off.

'I don't know how he did it,' I said, looking from face to face. 'But it has to be him.'

'Why?' Jiri asked.

'The boys in Accident Inquiry have just finished their examination of the piece of fuel pipe I found – '

'And?' Lilo said before I could finish.

'And judging from the section it was cut from and the angle of the cuts, whoever did it was left-handed. Jack's checked records. Marc Desmoulins is the only left-handed person on the base.'

The words were hardly out of my mouth before Jiri had called Security and told them to arrest Marc Desmoulins and charge him with murder.

A few minutes later they buzzed back.

'He's not in his room, sir. There's a note on his bed – '

'What does it say?' snapped Jiri.

'It's addressed to Jack Nairn,' we heard the guard say.

'Read it!' Jiri's voice was tense.

We heard the sound of an envelope being ripped open, then, 'Dear Jack, I've just been summoned to Jiri Kun's office. I know they think I killed Lars Aschengreen. If I get out of the interrogation without being charged, I'm off straight away. There must be a way I can prove I'm innocent and I'll stay in hiding till I can think what it is. Yours, Marc.'

'Raise the alarm,' thundered Jiri. 'I want him found.'

'He can't have gone far,' said Lilo. 'He must still be in the building somewhere.'

'Sir!' Another voice echoed down the line. 'Transport Security have just reported that Desmoulins has stolen a rocketcar. He's out of the 'sphere and was last seen heading for the *Valles*

Marineris.'

'We'll never find him if he gets there,' said Frederic Mann. 'That place is riddled with canyons and caverns. It would be like looking for a rat in the rainforest.'

'He won't last long even if he does get there,' said Lilo. 'He doesn't have any supplies.'

'We don't know that for sure,' said Jiri. 'He had all night to arrange something.'

'I'm going after him,' I said, jumping to my feet.

'Don't be silly, Stravinsky.' Jiri shook his head. 'He's driving the fastest thing on four wheels and he's got a head start on you.'

'Sir,' I said. 'This is my assignment. And if I take a spacecab, not only is it faster, I may be able to spot him from the air.'

'Very well,' said Jiri. 'But I'm starting a full-scale search as well. Oh, and take Nairn with you.'

A few minutes later Jack and I were in the air, zooming towards *Valles Marineris*, the largest and deepest canyon system so far found in the solar system. We were flying low with a strong wind on my tail and were making good progress when suddenly Jack shouted, 'There's a dust storm up ahead. We're going to have to land.'

'What, and get trapped in the dust?'

'There's a huge rock over there,' Jack pointed to his right. 'If we shelter in its lee, we'll be all right.'

'OK,' I nodded. 'Fasten your seat belt. It's gonna be a bumpy ride.'

Bumpy wasn't the word for it.

By the time we were on the ground and had come to a halt by the rock, I felt as if I'd been on the rollercoaster ride of a lifetime.

'Just as well I only had coffee for breakfast,' gulped Jack. 'Anything else would have come back up for an encore.'

Sitting in the safety of the spacecab with the dust swirling by was like being on an island in the middle of a hurricane.

'How long is this thing going to last?' I asked after what seemed like hours.

'It's blowing itself out now,' said Jack. 'Look!'

Sure enough, the thick red dustclouds were thinning out, changing before our eyes to puffs of scarlet powder being blown along by a gentle breeze.

'Put it on vertical take-off and let's get going,' I ordered.

'I hope Marc found somewhere to shelter,' Jack said a few minutes later when we were back in the air. 'I'd hate to think of him suffocating in all that dust.'

'Even if what he did resulted in the deaths of four men?' I asked.

'You've no actual proof it was him.' Jack stressed the word 'actual'.

'Oh come on, Jack,' I smiled. 'The pipe was cut by a left-hander. Marc's the only one on the base. Putting two and two together, I'd say that made four, wouldn't you?'

'I guess so,' said Jack. 'I just want to ask him why. Why did three innocent men have to die so he could get revenge on Aschengreen?'

'Looks like you won't have long to wait,' I said. 'For unless I'm very much mistaken, that's his rocket-car down there.'

CHAPTER 20

'I'll take the controls,' I said. 'Switch over.'

As soon as Jack keyed in the command, I took the spacecab down very low and accelerated until I was flying directly above the rocketcar.

We hovered there for a moment or two before accelerating again.

The spacecab shot past Marc's car and when it was five or six hundred metres in front, I turned her 180 degrees. Then, clinging to the ground, I headed straight for Marc, taking the 'cab up a split second before were about to crash.

I heard a groan from my left. 'That was so close,' Jack gulped. 'We must have almost scratched his roof.'

'You ain't seen nothing yet,' I said through gritted teeth, once again turning the plane on its tracks and heading back on Marc's tail. But this time when I had caught up with him, I stayed so close behind him and so low to the ground that the spacecab's nose glowed in the heat of the rocketcar's hot exhaust gases.

'I think I'm about to say hello to my coffee again,' Jack retched as Marc threw the car first to the left then to the right, zigzagging madly all over the place. The cloud of dust he was throwing up was so thick I had to take the spacecab up so I could see where I was going.

'We're heading straight for that cliff!' yelled Jack. 'Look out!'

I tugged so hard on the thrust director controls that I thought the 'cab would flip backwards.

But it didn't.

When we were ten metres from the rockface, the 'cab shot straight upwards with a deafening shriek.

'Thank goodness – ' But before Jack could finish what he was going to say, the spacecab was shaken by a loud explosion from below. A moment later we were shrouded in a cloud of red dust.

'What the hell?' I cried, struggling to steady the plane.

'It's Marc,' Jack shouted. 'He must have crashed into the cliff.'

'Look!' I said a few moments later when the dust had started to clear. 'He ejected!'

We both watched as the rocketcar's ejector seat, with Marc Desmoulins safely strapped into it, floated gently downwards.

* * * * *

'Well done, Stravinsky.' Jiri shook my hand and even Lilo Gruber smiled, if you can call an obviously forced upward turning of the lips a smile.

'What'll happen to him?' asked Matz Borlin.

'He'll be sent back to Earth to stand trial,' said Jiri. 'We now have motive and evidence, thanks to DeeDee.'

'Evidence?' said Frederic Mann.

'Yes,' I nodded. 'I was thinking of the case as a jigsaw which we've fitted together piece by piece. But there was a bit I couldn't complete.'

'What was that?' asked Lilo.

'We know the fuel pipe was cut, and we're sure it was Desmoulins who cut it, right?'

Everyone nodded.

'So?' Lilo puckered her pug-like little face.

'So as Frederic pointed out, how come the shuttle didn't explode when it took off from here? Why did it blow up the second time it took off? From *Olympus Mons*? Not when it took off from here? Until I knew that, I couldn't finish the jigsaw.'

'And?'

'The only way would have been to block the main fuel pipe with a slow-dissolving resin. The fuel would have automatically diverted to the back-up system until the resin dissolved, something Aschengreen or one of the others should have noticed during countdown. We'll never know why he didn't.'

'Maybe he did notice, but didn't want to delay his mission,' said Jiri. 'Time was tight and the back-up supply system is one hundred per cent efficient.'

I was pleased to see everyone nod.

'I had the piece of pipe analysed last night and sure enough, there are minute traces of just such a resin on it.'

'Why wasn't this spotted earlier?' No prizes for guessing who asked that.

'It's not a standard test,' I replied and went on, 'After I got the results, I had a rummage in Desmoulins' quarters and came across a pack of the resin.'

'Where was it?' asked Jack who had been specially invited to attend the meeting.

'In his tennis bag,' I shrugged my shoulders. 'In a computer disk box.'

Jack frowned.

'What's so puzzling?' I asked.

'But I had his tennis bag,' Jack said. 'Until after Marc was arrested last night. After we finished our game two nights ago we went for something to eat. We got caught up with Hilly King's birthday party. Marc left before me and forgot his bag.'

'So how come it was in his room?' Jiri's eyes narrowed as he spoke.

'I took it there when Dee D– er – Miss Stravinsky and I got home last night,' Jack said. 'There was no disk box in that bag. I know for sure because I thought his spare smart card might have been in the bag. I rummaged for it so I could get into his room to put the bag back.'

'How did you get in,' Lilo asked, 'without a smart card?'

'The security officer guarding the door let me in,' Jack said. 'She came in with me. Someone must have put the resin in the bag after I left it there.'

'Security records will show who went in,' said Jiri, staring at me.

'Someone get me a can of Cola,' I said, shifting uncomfortably in my seat.

'Here,' said Frederic Mann who had gone to Jiri's fridge to get himself a glass of iced water. 'Catch.'

Frederic must have been at the back of the class when they were giving throwing lesson. The can flew across the room and was just about to flash by my left side when without thinking what I was doing I reached out and caught it.

'Great catch,' said Jack. 'Didn't know you were

ambidextrous.'

'Right hand, left hand, it doesn't matter to me. I can use bo– ' I stopped before I finished the word.

A murmur echoed around the room.

'I think', said Jiri in an ice-cold voice, '. . . you may have something to tell us, Stravinsky.'

* * * * *

I had the motive – ever since the day my dad had died I had blamed Lars Aschengreen for his death. And when he had told me that if the Deimos experiment failed he was going to commit the Agency to carrying on my father's work, I had been cold with fury. If he'd backed Dad at the very beginning, the accident would never have happened and Dad would still be alive today. And that made me hate Aschengreen so much I didn't care how many others died along with him, as long as I had my revenge.

I had the opportunity – as Head of Rocketry and Rocket Research I was in and out of the launch area so often the security guards hardly noticed me. It had taken less than a minute to cut the pipe and block the area just above with the resin. I knew exactly how long it would take for it to dissolve. I knew precisely when the fuel would surge through from the back-up supply and leak out the gap I had cut.

I even had the suspect all lined up. I knew that

Cooper hated Aschengreen and why. Dad had known him and told me. If Jack hadn't spotted the connection, I would have pretended to.

I also knew he'd kept a diary. Dad had told me that, too. 'Puts down everything.'

I'd been one hundred per cent sure I wouldn't ever be caught.

Being asked to lead the investigation had made me two hundred per cent sure.

How was I to know Aschengreen would leave behind the very lifeboat I had dropped the piece of pipe in? I expected it to be blown up along with everything else on board when the shuttle exploded.

How could I possibly have known about Simon Cooper's illness? There was no way I could have known he couldn't have cut the pipe.

How was I to know Jiri would ask me to take Jack Nairn along? Good old, eagle-eyed, high-flying Jack Nairn. If he hadn't spotted the piece of pipe in the lifeboat, no one would ever have known about it. I could easily have covered up the fact that the pipe had been cut.

I confessed – there was no point in trying to deny it.

I'd broken the eleventh commandment – I'd caught myself out.

THE RED PLANET

Mars is the planet that glows red in the night sky. At times, it is the third brightest object there, after the Moon and Venus. It is the fourth planet from the Sun, and the next beyond Earth. One-and-a-half times farther from the Sun than the Earth, Mars revolves round the Sun once every 687 days.

Its atmosphere is made up of 95.3 per cent carbon dioxide, 2.7 per cent nitrogen and 1.6 per cent argon, with only traces of oxygen. The surface pressure on the planet is one per cent that of the Earth's and gravity is one-third of our planet's.

The surface temperature varies from a chilling -128°C (-199°F) at the poles during the night to a pleasant 17°C (63°F) at midday on the equator.

In the early 1990s NASA announced two missions to Mars – *Mars Pathfinder* and *Mars Global Surveyor*. They were both launched in 1996.

Both had their roots in two separate NASA programmes. *Pathfinder* was a one-off project, part of NASA's *Discovery* programme. This was created in 1992 to fund inexpensive missions to the solar system. Inexpensive in terms of space research, that is. The budget for *Pathfinder* was around $200 million.

The mission was a triumph. The pictures and other nuggets of information sent back thrilled NASA scientists and gave them masses of new information about the planet.

Global Surveyor was the first of a series of missions aimed at surveying Mars over ten years or more. Each mission involves sending two spacecraft – one to go into orbit around the planet, the other to land on it – during the periods in 1996, 1998, 2001, 2003 and 2005 when Mars and the Earth are closest to each other.

The first of these missions, *Surveyor '96*, sent back valuable information about the Martian atmosphere and the planet's magnetic field.

Surveyor '98 Orbiter was launched on 10 December 1998. Its mission when it reaches Mars is to send back more information about the atmosphere, establish if there is moisture in it, and if so to find out if the amount varies much.

It will also be used to beam signals from the *Lander*, which was launched on 3 January 1999. Its mission is to assess past and present-day water resources on the planet, study weather conditions, the shape of the landscape, and mineral supplies.

The 2001 and 2003 missions will continue this work, preparing the way for the 2005 mission. This is the one when NASA hopes to bring back actual rock samples from the surface of the Red Planet.

STEP BY STEP

Here's how some NASA scientists see the various stages that will lead to human beings living on Mars.

Stage 1 Advanced exploration of the planet's surface and atmosphere. NASA's *Global Surveyor* programme has already started this.

Stage 2 Robotic surface exploration. This began with Pathfinder's *Sojourner Rover* and will continue in future *Mars Surveyor* missions.

Stage 3 Initial human expeditions. At some time in the next century, five men and women will clamber into a single-stage, radiation-proof, nuclear/solar-powered spacecraft and get ready to journey to Mars.

Their spaceship will have been assembled on board the International Space Station. The first parts of this were launched in 1998 and work on the station will continue for many years to come.

When the Martian spacecraft is ready, it will be put into Earth orbit. The crew will then use a space shuttle to journey from Earth to board it. This is much cheaper than blasting off directly from Earth.

After around 510 days in space, the spacecraft will reach Mars. The crew will then spend 39 days manoeuvring it around the planet to get it into the exact position to put it into fixed orbit 3,000 kilometres above the planet's surface.

The spacecraft will stay there for a 100-day reconnaissance mission. During this time three of the crew will land on the planet's surface and spend 30 days there before transferring back to the mother ship and heading for home.

Stage 4 Development of the Martian resource base. It could be many decades before permanent settlements are established on Mars. Before that, sophisticated robots will have been put to work to prepare sites on which humans will live and work.

The first Martian habitats will be modules built on the International Space Station and ferried to Mars aboard nuclear-electric cargo propulsion ships. Once on the planet, these modules will be positioned and interconnected as necessary. Then they will be covered with at least a metre of Martian soil. This is to protect them from the lethal effects of radiation produced by solar flares and cosmic rays; for Mars has no thick atmosphere to act as a radiation shield.

The settlements will be small at first. Each one will probably house no more than ten people. These pioneers will spend their time exploring the planet and finding out what resources are available.

Once the first colonists have established themselves, work will begin on engineering projects using native Martian materials.

Later, industries will be established on Mars and the bases will grow. At first this will be a slow process but as more and more people go to live and work on the planet the pace will quicken. Bigger bases will be built, some housing as many as 1,000 people. Then the bases will be built closer and closer to each other and small towns will be created.

At the same time as the settlements are growing, more and more Martian resources will be used. Food will be grown on the planet. Martian fuels will be used. Mining expeditions will take off from Mars to exploit the mineral-rich asteroid belt between Mars and Jupiter, the next planet out in the Solar System.

THE MARS AEROPLANE

NASA is already considering building unmanned aeroplanes to help them explore Mars. Made of lightweight carbon-fibre composites, the aeroplanes will weigh less than 50 kilograms.

The wings, fuselage and tail section will fold away. This will allow the aeroplane to be stowed in an 'aircraft carrier', which will parachute the aeroplane from Martian orbit down towards the planet's surface. When it has reached the height at which scientists want it to fly, the craft's fifteen-horsepower hydrazine airless engine will automatically start up and the parachutes will fall away.

Then, flying at between 500 metres and fifteen kilometres, the Martian aeroplane will photograph the surface and conduct various surveys.